MORE SCIENCE FICTION BY KRISTINE KATHRYN RUSCH

THE DIVING UNIVERSE

Series Reading Order

Diving into the Wreck: A Diving Novel

City of Ruins: A Diving Novel

Becalmed: A Diving Universe Novella

The Application of Hope: A Diving Universe Novella

Boneyards: A Diving Novel

Skirmishes: A Diving Novel

The Runabout: A Diving Novel

The Falls: A Diving Universe Novel

Searching for the Fleet: A Diving Novel

The Spires of Denon: A Diving Universe Novella

The Renegat: A Diving Universe Novel

Escaping Amnthra: A Diving Universe Novella

The Court-Martial of the Renegat Renegades

Thieves: A Diving Novel

Squishy's Teams: A Diving Universe Novel

The Chase: A Diving Novel

Ivory Trees: A Diving Universe Novel

Maelstrom: A Diving Universe Novella

——— ••• ———

THE RETRIEVAL ARTIST SERIES

The Disappeared

Extremes

Consequences

Buried Deep

Paloma

Recovery Man

The Recovery Man's Bargain

Duplicate Effort

The Possession of Paavo Deshin

Anniversary Day

Blowback

A Murder of Clones

Search & Recovery

The Peyti Crisis

Vigilantes

Starbase Human

Masterminds

The Impossibles

The Retrieval Artist

———— ••• ————

STANDALONE SCIENCE FICTION NOVELS

Alien Influences

Snipers

SCIENCE FICTION COLLECTIONS

Colliding Worlds, Vol. 1

Colliding Worlds, Vol. 2

Colliding Worlds, Vol. 3

Colliding Worlds, Vol. 4

Colliding Worlds, Vol. 5

Colliding Worlds, Vol. 6

WEATHER DUTY

A SCIENCE FICTION NOVELLA

KRISTINE KATHRYN RUSCH

WMG PUBLISHING

CONTENTS

WEATHER DUTY

WEATHER DUTY

AMALA NAVARRO PULLED one of the damp wipes from the dispenser above the counter, and wiped the sweat off her face. She'd had to walk the last few blocks in the 110-degree heat because the light rail broke down for the fifth time this week. At least they'd managed to get the doors open. The last time, the doors stayed shut and rescuers had to smash their way in—taking nearly a dozen cars out of commission at a time when the city needed them most.

She wished she had brought another outfit. She would have slipped into the restroom and removed her shirt and matching leggings, so no one saw just how sweat-covered she was. She had chosen the outfit to impress her new colleagues, not thinking about how much the thin gray material showed the littlest stain—and her sweat stains from that light rail incident were not little.

At least she had her water bottle. She'd managed to refill that as she entered City Hall after realizing the bottle was empty while she was standing in the security line.

What a day. What a horrible start to her brand-new civic duty.

At least she had arrived—fifteen minutes early—at the bland little room in a not-so-bland building. City Hall had been one of the first buildings in Las Vegas to be certified energy efficient. Its solar pipes and panels were ancient— particularly by local standards—built in the teens. But they were still effective and more important, they were *pretty*.

Light blue and gray panels formed trees in the plaza and the building itself had lovely windows that captured the sun. Older buildings weren't usually this beautiful, but somehow City Hall managed to hold up.

She had expected every room to have windows. The windows might have overlooked Civic Plaza or all the casinos on Fremont Street, but at least they would have had a view.

This meeting room didn't have a view and was smaller than she expected. It seemed even more narrow than it was because of the counters that lined the wall as well as the long table in the middle that was too big for the space. Someone had placed fake ferns in the corners, and all four ferns were fluttering slightly, so at least the room had air movement.

The ferns were an unusual bit of whimsy in an aggressively brown and tan room. The tiled floor was dark brown; the walls were a lighter brown. The counters were dark brown too, so that from some angles, they disappeared against the tile floor.

The table was the same dark brown, which made it seem to grow out of that floor. Only a handful of the chairs matched. Those had tan cushions and straight backs. Other chairs had clearly been dragged into the room to reach the number of seats needed. Those newer chairs were a startling silver. They were somewhat modern, and might (she heard herself mentally stressing *might)* have comfort modifications so that the chair would conform to whomever sat in it.

She looked at those chairs in dismay. Every time she'd encountered those when she did her civic duty, it meant that the commission she was on was expected to work long hours.

She hoped that these chairs had arrived only because of a seating shortage and not because she was going to spend her entire July in this room.

She tossed the used wipe in the recycler near the door, grabbed another wipe, and scrubbed off aggressively. The air conditioning had been set at the mandated 75 degrees, which she normally found comfortable, but on this day, it seemed much too high. That walk had really sapped her energy.

Doing anything in July was crazy, particularly in the years when it was a mandated "average" month, like this year. Average high temperatures here in Las Vegas in July hovered around 110, but the programmers always added a few degrees in either direction, particularly at the beginning and end of the month, just to make sure no one could easily predict the weather.

She had no idea why an easy prediction was something to be avoided. But she hadn't been around when the system had been designed, so she had no say in the requirements.

She was going to have a say in the weather, though, because that was what the Weather Commission did. The commission was pretty controversial because everyone had an opinion about the weather, and none of those opinions were the same. The manual she had received describing her duties had been clear on that point:

Everyone from your family to random strangers will tell you what the weather should be. Some shadier characters will try to influence your weather decisions. Hold fast and make decisions based on what is best for the Las Vegas Valley. Report any untoward conversations to the chair of the commission or Las Vegas Metro Police.

That last line had initially sent a shiver through her. If that part of the manual hadn't been clear enough, another part, which was repeated in red throughout and would literally lift above any page she was reading, stated:

Anyone accepting bribes or other forms of influence during their service at the Weather Commission will be punished to the fullest extent of the law.

That phrase was repeated in the videos she had watched and even in the cheesy game she had been required to play (using ancient and provided "virtual reality" software) that simulated a week in the life of a commissioner.

She had never had to do simulated service before actual service in all her years of civic duty, and it had unnerved her.

Apparently the Civic Duty Authority of the Las Vegas Valley took the Weather Commission a lot more seriously than she had expected when she signed up.

She stared at the chairs like they were her enemies. If she picked one of the comfort chairs, she was acknowledging that the Weather Commission owned her for the next several hours. If she picked one of the ancient chairs and the meeting did go on forever, she was dooming herself to backaches and discomfort.

She wiped a hand over her clammy forehead. Yes, she was overthinking this. But, she finally realized, she was scared.

She had never been scared of her civic duty before, although she probably should have been. Fresh out of college, she had been assigned to the Public Health

Commission. Everyone on that commission had been serious and dedicated, many of them three times her age.

They followed the latest science, made decisions in a bloodless manner, and talked in generic terms such as *Is fifteen percent an acceptable loss?* It had taken her nearly a week on that commission before she realized that they meant a 15% loss of *life*.

It wasn't the bloodlessness that had gotten to her, though. It had been the descriptions of pathogens or different types of contamination. The oldest on the commission—and the most fanatical—had lived through the Covid crisis of the early 20s, and had vowed to never let any future generation repeat that experience. Initially Amala had liked each of her colleagues, but over time, the older ones, who seemed to react to everything with fear and anger, unnerved her almost as much as the images of what certain biological agents could do to the human body.

When she first became eligible for a transfer to a new commission, she applied. It had taken two years to get off the Public Health Commission, which meant she had ultimately put seven years into the place.

Seven years I'll never get back, she had told her friends one drunken Friday evening. They had looked at her without sympathy. Everyone had to do their civic duty. The system had been designed when it became clear that elected officials were more interested in their political careers then they were in the nitty-gritty of governing.

In many, many essential services, gridlock caused increased illness and death. Those services were removed from the political landscape by the Civic Duty Laws passed nationwide before she was born. Each community got to designate their own civic duty commissions, with the CDA mandating certain commissions nationwide. Public Health had been part of the CDA from the beginning; Weather got its own national designation after the passage of climate laws and a change in technology made it possible for certain regions to actually control the weather within their borders.

She had thought Weather would be interesting. She could still use her science background, and she wouldn't be subject to images of biophages that ate human flesh.

But standing here, in this bland, empty room, she felt a lot of trepidation. Maybe she had made the wrong choice after all.

She hovered, resisting the urge to pull out her designated phone. The phone had been given to her when she joined this commission. Personal tech shut down inside this part of City Hall for legal and governmental reasons; that was why so many commission meetings were held here. The phone was given to her so that she could record the meeting (apparently, she needed the legal protection, which also made her nervous) and so that she could contact friends and family if need be.

She had programmed the phone the week before the meeting, and had had a sudden moment of panic as the names turned red after she inputted them. Red meant the names were unacceptable to the system. After a long five minutes, though, her contact list was approved.

Apparently, they all had to be vetted and the old tech had taken an impossibly long time to verify each contact she had put in.

She had a hunch she would have to get used to weird requirements and impossibly long wait times. She had thought Public Health was paranoid—and they were—but they were paranoid about what might happen to the city, the county, or the state should something evil (the word used by the oldsters) get loose.

Weather seemed to be paranoid about everything.

She looked at her watch—which was missing, of course, because she wasn't allowed to wear it here. The watch kept all but the most personal data for her; she had gotten the required implant with all of her identification embedded as well as the emergency contact information, but she had so hated the experience that she didn't want to have any more. Hence the watch. The *missing* watch.

She supposed she could ask the room for the time or pull out her phone and check, but she didn't want to appear nervous. Although there was a chance she was in the wrong location, and she wasn't exactly sure how she could figure that out.

At that moment the door opened, and a harried elderly woman entered. The woman had had no augmentations. Her face was leathery—the kind of Vegas leathery that came from spending too much time in the sun without the proper amount of protection. Her white hair was thin and revealed age-spots on the top of her scalp.

She wore a loose blue canvas dress and carried a sweater over her arm. To Amala's dismay, the woman did not look like she had been in the heat at all.

"Oh," the woman said, her voice going down with disappointment. "A newbie. Amala, right?"

"Yes," Amala said.

"There will be two of you. Newbies, that is. Not Amalas. Although we did have two Luises once. That was annoying." The woman rolled her eyes, then glared at Amala. "Try not to slow down the meeting with too many process questions. We have a lot to cover."

Amala felt her tension increase. At Public Health, the first hour of the first meeting of the month was given over to explaining procedure to the newbies. It was a courtesy that saved time, or so she had been told.

She wondered how on earth she would understand what to do in this commission if no one explained the standard stuff.

But the woman no longer met her gaze. The woman had made her way to the back of the room, and set her sweater on one of the comfy chairs. Then she removed one of the matching chairs from the head of the table and replaced it with the chair she had claimed. She sat down heavily, reached into a canvas bag that had so matched her outfit that Amala hadn't noticed it before, and pulled out an old-fashioned tablet.

She placed it on the table with such force that the table protested. Immediately a group of warnings rose: *No Personal Items Allowed! Power Down Devices! Do Not Place Beverages On The Table!* . . . and Amala's immediate favorite: *This Is A Working Table, Not A Relaxing Table.*

Duly noted. Even the table was cranky in this room. She tried not to smile.

"Ignore those," the woman said, waving her hand at them. "They will disappear shortly. It's a glitch in the system that no one seems to want to fix."

She tucked a wisp of white hair behind one surprisingly pink ear and said, "Oh, by the way, in case you hadn't figured it out, I'm Mirabelle. I am the lucky person who is the chair of this commission for two more years and counting."

"Nice to meet you," Amala said. She was too far away to offer a hand to shake, and besides, Mirabelle looked like she was of the generation that looked at any personal contact with great suspicion.

"Sit, sit," Mirabelle said. "We will be starting in five minutes."

Amala glanced at the empty chairs in surprise. It had always taken Public Health a good fifteen minutes to settle in before anyone officially started the meeting.

"I'm not kidding," Mirabelle said. "Pick your chair. This is probably your last chance."

Amala normally would have sat near the back, but that was where Mirabelle was sitting, and Amala just didn't want to be close. She didn't want to be noticed either, and she wasn't quite sure how to accomplish both in this room. Finally, she picked the comfy chair in the right corner closest to the door. She had her back to one of the counters, but that didn't bother her as much as having her back to the door would have.

She sat down gingerly, feeling a familiar buzz against her legs, as the chair commanded her to settle in. It couldn't perform its magic if she didn't sit properly. Some older chairs actually announced that.

She scooted the chair closer to the table so that there would be enough room for people to pass behind her, then eased toward the back of the chair. At that moment, the buzzing stopped, and the chair molded itself to her thighs and buttocks. If she got uncomfortable, all she had to do was shift and the chair would readjust.

At least it was a comfort chair in good working order. In the past, she had sat in some of these old models that had lost a good half of their functionality, which made them even more uncomfortable than so-called regular chairs.

"Phone on the table," Mirabelle said. She wasn't even looking up. She was scrolling through that ancient tablet. "In theory, the table will synch up and you can get all the minutes. In practice, doublecheck about fifteen minutes in. Sometimes this old tech does what it wants, and that isn't always what we want."

Amala swallowed hard. She hated first days of anything. The first day at Public Health had been particularly scary. Her parents and siblings had always complained about their civic duty months, and she had worried about hers.

There, at Public Health, the chair had explained that they would be making decisions that impacted the lives of millions of people, so each commissioner had to take their duties seriously. Amala had taken hers seriously, even though she hadn't liked it. And because of the nature of that commission, she couldn't even bitch about her service.

Public Health had the most stringent non-disclosure agreements of all of the commissions. Weather's was surprisingly light. It had the usual penalties for revealing what occurred at meetings without the chair's permission, but lacked the higher level penalties of Public Health. There, if she had violated, she would have received an automatic five years in jail.

Here, if she violated, she would be subject to fines—albeit massive ones.

Fines were more than good enough to dissuade her. She didn't have a lot of money. She had stumbled into a low-paying job she loved at one of the performance studios. She was a junior choreographer and had already worked on a dozen different shows in casinos on the Las Vegas Strip. The job was flexible, and her hours were often on nights and weekends, especially when a show was in rehearsals.

That was why she felt she could do three months civic duty service, so she could graduate from civic duty at 50 instead of at 70, like everyone else. She had been the one to sign up for July (stupidly). She had also chosen December, since the city mostly closed down before Christmas. The third month was to be determined, depending on when the commission needed an experienced member . . . which she was not yet.

She was beginning to wonder if this was a mistake. Maybe she should have stayed with Public Health. The meetings there were easy and understandable, even if they were often grim.

Here . . .

The door opened and four more people spilled in. Two were men, one with a cowboy hat that he kept on as he walked toward Mirabelle in the back. A faint odor of horses rose off of him as he passed behind Amala.

The other man took a seat across from her. He was too thin and balding, his shirt baggy and a bit frayed. Amala knew that some people sat on several commissions simply for the rather meager income, because they couldn't get jobs anywhere else.

She hoped he was not one of them.

The other two seemed joined at the hip. They looked

too young to be on this commission, but she had learned that appearances, particularly youthful ones, meant nothing in this town. She couldn't determine gender, either, which took away an easy way to identify them.

They walked together to the back of the room too, and sat—almost in unison—kitty-corner across from Amala.

That was six. There should be five more. As the manual said, an uneven number on the commission guaranteed there would be no tie votes. Everyone knew it didn't really happen that way, but it was a good theory.

No one really looked at Amala. No one greeted her. No one said anything about her being new.

It was so different from Public Health that she had no idea how to behave. She had been warned, back when she had civic duty training straight out of college, that on some commissions, the permanent members often saw the citizen commissions as interlopers.

She hadn't encountered that at Public Health, but maybe that was the case here.

All she knew was that the Weather Commission, unlike Public Health, only had three permanent members. Mirabelle was one because she was the chair. Amala hoped the others would be introduced when the meeting started.

The permanent members were often the interface between the commission and whatever agency it oversaw. The commission functioned like a governing board. Some commissions even had a few non-voting members, people from the agency who sat in on each meeting. The agency people sometimes acted as advisors, and sometimes as conduits between the agency and the commission on a daily basis, instead of the biweekly basis mandated by law.

At Public Health, the agency people often explained the science, and were often the ones who had the scariest and/or grossest things to say. The agency people were useful, though, so that someone with an ancient biology degree didn't commandeer the meeting and pretend that they were the expert.

Amala didn't see any agency people yet, nor did she see a place for them to sit. There were just eleven chairs around this table, which meant that there was no room for any kind of monitors.

She fidgeted and the chair froze, its soft curves suddenly hard. It was probably waiting to see if she was going to permanently switch position.

She had forgotten just how annoying these chairs could be.

The door opened again, and a heavyset man staggered in. He carried a suitcoat over his arm and his entire shirt was sweat-stained. He tossed his coat on one of the chairs —mercifully far from Amala—and then said, "Oh, good. We're not all here yet. I'm going to change my shirt," and walked back out the door.

At least she wasn't the only one who had suffered in the morning's heat.

Mirabelle's mouth thinned. She looked annoyed. The man in the cowboy hat rolled his eyes, but no one else said anything.

The door didn't really have a chance to close before an older man walked in. His back was bent and his gait was slow. He appeared to be older than Mirabelle. He nodded at everyone and headed to Mirabelle's side.

If Amala had to guess, and right now, that was all she could do, she would have guessed that he was another of the permanent members.

Two women came in, both laughing, although the laughter stopped as they stepped inside. Unlike the earlier couple, these two did not sit next to each other. They both wore black dresses and heels, so they must have come from somewhere nearby.

No one except attorneys and government officials wore black downtown in the summer.

Finally, one more man entered. He was tall, with muscular arms peeking out of a tight t-shirt that covered very broad shoulders. His black hair was mussed, his jeans professionally pressed, and his red-and-black shoes so expensive that Amala could live off of the amount he spent on them for two years straight.

He scanned the room, as if he expected to meet some-one. As she watched him, she had a nagging sense she knew who he was.

Working on the Las Vegas Strip had attuned her to that feeling. Celebrities often looked different in person, but something about them would strike a chord anyway. She never wanted to fan-girl at any of them, but she always liked knowing who she was dealing with.

That was one of the things that irritated her about Public Health and now here: she never got names ahead of time. She had no idea who she was working with until she got there.

It would be different here. The manual said that people who were on the Weather Commission could use their first names in the meeting only.

Which suddenly made her wonder how they had handled the two-Luis situation.

The familiar guy hovered near the door. "Is this the Weather Commission?" he asked in a slightly strangled tone.

The strangle wasn't enough to disguise his voice. Amala had heard it a million times in videos, movies, shows, and narrations all over the web. This man was Ezra Oliver, who had moved to Las Vegas two years before when he started a residency on the Strip.

She had heard that celebrities had to perform civic duty as well, but she had never seen any on Public Health. The fact that they had had to perform civic duty —all over the country, not just in the Vegas Valley— was why so few of them had permanent addresses anymore. There was a new bill in Congress to get rid of that loophole and it looked like it was going to go through since members of Congress had to perform civic duty if they ever retired from their work in government.

Some celebrities were trying to find a new loophole. Most of them who wanted permanent addresses had them in a community that allowed civic duty to be transferred to another person, which let the celebrity pay an exorbitant amount of money for someone to take their place. Most of those places, though, were not anywhere that a celebrity wanted to live. Miami had the best benefits, but most of the city was underwater, and it smelled awful, as she learned when she had gone on her one and only dance tour.

The Vegas Valley followed the same rules as New York, Los Angeles and Seattle. If a celebrity lived in the valley, they had to perform their civic duty—and they couldn't get out of it.

Mirabelle hadn't even looked up when Ezra spoke. She continued tapping on her ancient tablet.

"Yes," she said in an impatient voice. "This is the Weather Commission. You must be Ez."

Seriously? Amala almost said. *Ez?* Because everyone had the option of making up a first name for this commission if they filed it with the Civic Duty Authority a month in advance. Maybe he had missed that detail or his people had somehow screwed up.

"Yes, I'm Ez." He looked trapped. Everyone else was watching him, everyone except Amala, because she didn't want him to see the recognition on her face.

"That makes you the other newbie." Mirabelle leaned back in her chair, and looked at him. Her eyebrows went up for a moment, but that was the only thing that showed she had recognized him.

He waited, maybe expecting her to say something about his fame.

Instead, she launched into the same annoyed speech she had given Amala, and ended with, "I'd prefer it if newbies don't ask a lot of questions. You'll pick it up as we go."

Ez nodded, and contemplated the chairs just like Amala had done. He could remove the sodden suitcoat from the only remaining comfy chair or he could take the straight-backed matching chair beside her.

He clearly opted for the path of least resistance, and sat down.

"I'm the other newbie," Amala whispered. "I'm Amala."

"Ez," he whispered back as if he hadn't given his name earlier. "What have I miss—"

"Let's not have crosstalk," Mirabelle said. "Crosstalk leads to alliances and alliances make our jobs ever so much more difficult."

Amala's cheeks heated. Ez nodded, and set his phone on the table, as instructed.

The group sat in silence while they waited for the heavyset man to return. He did a moment later, wearing a bright pink shirt that was a little too loose. It tied at the wrists and had strings down the front.

"You are officially late, Luis," Mirabelle said.

"And you are a pain in my rear, Mirabelle," the heavyset man—apparently one of the two Luises—said. "I had to go down to the first floor to grab my bag, not that it helped much. This was the only extra shirt I had left."

"Let me guess," the scrawny man in the frayed shirt said. "From the *Pirates of Penzance* Cabaret?"

"You know better, Wally," Mirabelle said. "No personal details. Not in the meetings."

The scrawny man—Wally—smiled at Luis in a way that people who shared a secret did. Luis did not seem to notice. He wandered around the table and grabbed his suitcoat, looking at it as if it offended him.

Then he tossed it behind him, as if it were a piece of garbage.

"Well, then, I guess we start talking about the heat," he said as he sat down. The chair he had commandeered—a comfy chair—groaned as if it didn't want to do its job. "Oh, great. You guys left me the broken chair."

"You were late," said one of the people that Amala had dubbed "The Twins" in her head.

"I was not late," Luis said, then pointed at Ez. "That guy came in after me."

"I had trouble finding the room," Ez said, his voice still strangled.

Amala wanted to tell him to talk normally. She wanted

to remind him that they had a month of meetings and he wouldn't be able to maintain that weird voice the whole time. But she didn't say anything. She was painfully aware that Mirabelle had twice expressed irritation at having newbies, and so Amala didn't want to call more attention to herself.

"Finding your way around here is not that hard," said the older man, half under his breath.

"Conrad," Mirabelle said, "don't antagonize."

"Too late," one of the women in the suits said cheerfully.

Amala folded her hands on her lap and wished she could disappear.

"I'm going to gavel this meeting to order," Mirabelle said, "and as such—"

"You don't have a real gavel," the older man, Conrad, said.

"You say that every time, Conrad," said the man in the cowboy hat with real annoyance.

"Because it bothers me," Conrad said.

"Then buy her a gavel or shut up," Cowboy Hat said.

"Crosstalk," Mirabelle said firmly. "Stop now."

Both men looked at her. Amala saw the kind of little boys they had once been, their jaws set in a *make-me* stance. The fact they weren't little boys was evident in the fact that they didn't say anything, apparently relying on looking stubborn and somewhat annoyed.

"I will explain a few things for the newbies and as a

reminder." Mirabelle stressed the word *reminder*, as if just having to use it bothered her.

Cowboy Hat rolled his eyes. Luis shook his head slightly, and Wally looked down at his hands. Ez sat very still beside Amala. It was amazing how a man that well known could actually disappear. If he hadn't been sitting beside her, she wouldn't have noticed him at all.

"We are a 5724-C3 Commission," Mirabelle said, enunciating the numbers slowly.

Amala knew vaguely what the numbers meant. The numbers were the section of federal law that established various kinds of commission. There were federal regulations on how each commission was conducted, the minimum it would pay its commissioners, and how it conducted some of its business.

"As such," Mirabelle said, "we do not have to meet for a required number of hours every month."

"We kno-o-w," one of the twins said just loud enough to be heard.

Mirabelle glared at the twin. "We have a job to finish each month. Once that job is finished, we are excused, which means—"

"We can have the whole month off if we're efficient," Wally said.

"Don't interrupt me, Wally," Mirabelle said.

"Sorry, Your Highness," Wally said. "It's just that we do know this crap, as Khai said."

"All except the newbies," Mirabelle said tightly. "As

you know from past experience, there's no guarantee they examined the manual and the pre-meeting materials."

"I did," Amala said.

"Me, too," Ez said.

Mirabelle gave them both a withering look. It took all of Amala's strength not to cringe. She had worked with some of the most difficult personalities in entertainment on the Strip. She couldn't let some woman on a local commission intimidate her into nothingness.

"Considering how many others over the years I've been on this commission had claimed that they too had examined all the assigned materials when they had not," Mirabelle said, looking more irritated as the conversation went on, "forgive me if I give your word the same respect I would give a bucket of warm piss."

"Mirabelle," said the other black-suited woman. "You promised. Respect, remember?"

"I conduct this commission my way, Luna," Mirabelle said. "You had your style when you were chair, I have mine."

"Got that," Luna said drily, and leaned back. She rested her heavily manicured right hand on the table, as if the movement would keep her calm.

"Because we have a task to finish," Mirabelle said, making eye contact with the people on the other side of the table from Amala, "the more time we waste in idle talk, back talk, or crosstalk, the less likely we are to finish quickly."

Amala nodded. That made sense to her. Ez hadn't moved at all.

"The problem, my dear newbies, are the months in which there are a lot of distractions from the commissioners and . . . or . . . a lot of materials that will come from our regional, national, and international partners. I don't know if you know, but we have to work together to approve major storms and out-of-district rains that could result in flooding for areas without a weather dome."

Amala had seen mentions like that in the manual, but little of it was explained. She also knew that there had been some controversy a few years back when a ghost town north of Las Vegas was nearly wiped away by what was called once-in-a-century rainfall.

The blame for that fell squarely on the Weather Commissions in the region, and on the Vegas Valley Weather Commission in particular. They had had to change their internal structure and get rid of several long-standing commissioners.

Amala hadn't heard any details other than those, but now she was curious. She wondered if she could look it all up when she got home.

"July is a particularly difficult month," Mirabelle said, "and not the best time for newbies. We have a lot to do."

"We always have a lot to do," Conrad muttered.

"Conrad, seriously," Mirabelle said. "I warned you last session that this kind of behavior might lead to a forced retirement."

"And I warned you that your bullying was going to get us all in trouble," he said.

"Conrad," said Cowboy Hat, "with all due respect, shut the fuck up."

Conrad's mouth twisted. He shook his head and shrugged, then leaned back in his chair.

Mirabelle rolled her eyes, letting her face express her irritation at that interruption. Then she looked directly at Amala and Ez and said, "Because your predecessors, including a few at this table I might add, refused to follow the pre-meeting instructions, I am making this request to you . . . Let the experienced members handle the bulk of the work on this commission. If you have questions, save them for the break or ask me privately, using your assigned phone. That way there will be a record."

Luna's long nails tapped on the table. The sound provoked a flare of the *This Is A Working Table, Not A Relaxing Table* warning, which made everyone look at Luna.

"Tell them what happened last July," Luna said.

Mirabelle's eyes narrowed. "It's not relevant."

"Oh, it is," Luna said. "I hit my term limit that June. You know that all chairs of all commissions are term-limited, right?"

Now Amala was getting irritated. Not only had she read the manual and the pre-meeting information, but she had served for years on another commission. Of course, she knew that chairs were term-limited. Of course she did.

"The practical result of that," Luna said, "was that last July was Mirabelle's first as chair."

A couple of people looked down. Conrad had a slight malicious smile on his face. Cowboy Hat had closed his eyes and was shaking his head.

"She decided that we needed to work as fast as possible. We had five newbies on the commission, the most allowed by law." Luna glanced at Mirabelle—and the look seemed vicious.

Mirabelle kept her hands on the tablet. "We don't need to—"

"Mirabelle got them to agree with her that July—*this July*, by the way—would be an average month," Luna said. "Of course, Mirabelle hadn't thought it through. I did try to explain it. She wouldn't let me talk."

"Oh, god," said the other twin, who, as far as Amala was concerned, was nameless. "This again."

"It's important," Luna said. "These newbies need to understand—"

"Here's the thing," the nameless twin said. "If you read the regulations, an average month is based on an average of the past fifty years, not on an average by all existing data. There's some word missing or something in the regional law, which is being litigated, by the way, and we're not going to get into it."

The nameless twin's tone had an edge to it, one that implied *Right? We're not going to talk more. Right?*

No one responded. Amala sat very still. She almost

didn't see Ez beside her, which meant that he was even more still than she was.

"The last fifty years," the nameless twin continued, "includes those killing heat domes of the twenties and early thirties, the ones that happened during the gridlock, before the commissions were even developed. So no one did anything, and the climate crisis—"

"Okay," Khai, the other twin said. "I suspect they get it."

Amala kinda did and she wasn't sure she liked it.

"Well, just to be clear," Luna said, "it means that the entire Vegas Valley is going to live with Mirabelle's mistake for the next thirty days."

"You could have explained things to me last year," Mirabelle muttered.

"I tried," Luna said. "You refused to listen."

"Can we not relitigate this entire mess?" the other woman in black said. "All I want to do is work on next July and then get the hell out of here."

Her words hung in the air for a moment. It seemed like no one knew how to start the conversation again or what to do with the meeting.

So Amala did what she always did in these situations. She took control and she placated.

"Um, speaking for myself," she said, "I promise to listen and ask questions only at the designated time. You all are the experts and I'm new to the commission, so I will keep quiet, learn, and contribute only when asked."

"Me, too," Ez said so hastily he forgot to modulate his voice.

Khai and the other woman in black looked at him sharply. His cheeks grew ever-so-slightly redder. He realized he had screwed up and they probably recognized him.

"Good," Mirabelle said. "Fine. Glad you understand."

She tapped the tablet again, and sighed. Everyone at the table seemed to stiffen, as if expecting something bad.

"All right," she said. "We have a lot on our plates, as those of you who were with us in June recall. The International Weather Commission mandated that we will start into an El Niño pattern in March and it will continue through February of the following year. Yes, for those of you who haven't been here since last July, the Southwest Region petitioned for a delay of the El Niño pattern and we lost. So we have to follow the international mandate and stay within its regulations. Does everyone follow?"

No, Amala wanted to say, finally understanding why Mirabelle did not want any questions. Amala had heard of weather patterns, and the manual had said that there were International Climate Summits which determined global patterns, designed to keep the planet healthy.

The manual had told her that in cheery tones, implying that if she liked her work on the local level, she could apply to rise in the ranks, working on the regional level, then on the national level, and if she was lucky, the international.

"Good," Mirabelle said when no one answered. "In that case . . ."

And she launched into so much jargon that Amala instantly felt lost. This had happened to her in Public Health as well, but she had been younger, more willing to assume the problem was hers and not the situation she was in.

The difference between then and now was pretty simple: she knew how to solve the problem now, and it wouldn't be using Mirabelle's method.

Amala began to make notes in her phone, vowing to bring her ancient assigned tablet next time. She would look up each word she didn't know, have some online expert explain the weather phenomenon to her and maybe take the approved classes listed in the manual so that she could follow along.

Because right now, the meeting had become—for her —mostly empty words combined with concepts she did not understand and a call for informed decision-making, which she clearly was not ready for.

She settled into her chair, glad she had chosen a comfy one, because she suspected that this meeting would consume its mandated minimums before anyone remembered that there were also required breaks.

———— ••• ————

WHEN THE MEETING finally ended—six long hours after it began—Amala staggered out of the main doors of City Hall. The temperature hovered around 112, according to the watch she had rescued from her new assigned storage locker. She had been ridiculously grateful to get that watch back.

She hadn't realized just how much it was a part of her until she hadn't had access to it for the bulk of the day.

Mirabelle had promised that the other three meetings each week would never last longer than two hours "provided everyone is prepared," which sounded like a threat. Everything that woman said sounded like a threat, or maybe that was just how Amala was responding after six hours of listening to droning details that she didn't entirely understand.

She found herself in the middle of the solar trees, which decades before had been the pride and joy of the city. The trees had grayish-white trunks that had to be cleaned by an actual person because of their age. Above the trunks were rectangular solar panels of a type that wasn't made anymore, tilted toward the Valley's prodigious sunlight.

After wending her way past the trees into Civic Plaza, she scurried into the shade provided by the north side of the City Hall Annex. No one sat on the tables in the little area between the Annex and the Civic Center; it was simply too hot.

She was covered in sweat again, just from that little

scurry. But that didn't force her indoors—not yet, anyway. After that meeting, she felt the urge to gaze upwards at the weather dome, something she hadn't done in a long, long time.

The dome wasn't completely visible from this vantage, because there were tall buildings blocking part of her view, but she had to look, since she'd been thinking about the dome all day.

The dome's thin surface was almost invisible during the day and impossible to see at night. The only reason the dome was visible at all during the day was because its surface sometimes glistened in the light, particularly when the dome cleaned itself. Those cleanings were more common in the spring and fall, as the outside weather changed.

The outside weather still influenced a lot, even if she didn't think about it much.

The winds were a good example. They coated the dome with dust, which was why it had to be cleaned so often in the spring and fall (and sometimes after a summer monsoon). But the Valley used to be subjected to prodigious winds with each seasonal weather change, winds that had become so destructive during the gridlock years that windows shattered and some poorly built buildings would blow apart, as if the valley had suffered through a hurricane or a tornado.

The dome still allowed winds—or maybe that was her new commission (she would have to check)—but they always stayed within mandated levels, and if the level was going to be high, citizens would start getting warnings weeks in advance.

She couldn't imagine being in out-of-control winds. The big storms—even in what used to be called Tornado Alley in the middle of the country—still hit, of course, but never had an impact on the human population. Or rarely, anyway. Sometimes an unusual death made it to the news, but only because that person had chosen to live outside of a weather dome.

She should have thought about all of this long before joining the commission. She hadn't really considered the weather, though. Weather happened every day, but choosing it, arguing over it, figuring out the highs and lows, that really hadn't struck her as something people did.

Unlike Public Health, which had seemed quite obvious to her. If biohazards got into the water supply, people died. If restaurants and groceries did not maintain certain standards of cleanliness, people died.

It wasn't until this excessively long meeting that she got reminded about the ways people could die in extreme weather.

Extreme weather was a curiosity now, not a part of daily life—at least for dome dwellers.

She was going to have to rethink all of that.

A bead of sweat ran down the small of her back. She needed to get inside or stand in the shade in the cooling area between the buildings on the far side of Civic Plaza. She couldn't remain out here much longer.

The problem wasn't so much the sunlight—the dome filtered the most harmful rays—but the "extreme and unnecessary heat" as Luna said later in the meeting. Mirabelle had responded that the heat wasn't as bad as unregulated heat outside the dome, and the meeting had devolved into fighting . . . again.

Amala itched to take over the meeting. She never allowed her dancers to talk like that. She would ban them from rehearsal if need be. And people in the arts were deemed temperamental. She was beginning to think that people in the arts weren't nearly as temperamental as people in government.

Or at least those who had their little fiefdoms inside the various commissions.

She sighed. After this first meeting, she really was regretting her choice. She should have stayed on Public Health, dealt with the icky stuff, and met for the designated eight hours per week for one month out of the year.

Served her right for trying to game the system. It seemed the system had gamed her.

She tapped her watch to see where the nearest public transport was. The live rail line she had taken here was back in service but running late. Maybe the smart move would be to get herself dinner at one of the nearby restaurants, using the last of her daily allowance for her civic duty service. That way, the sun would be down, and the heat would have faded a little, making the walk just a bit more comfortable.

"I thought I recognized you."

She jumped at the sound of the voice, which came from behind her. She pivoted, the voice lodging in her brain before she realized who she was talking to. Ez had crossed the plaza, looking cool and unruffled despite the heat.

She smiled at him tentatively. "Some meeting, huh?"

"Yeah. Too bad we can't discuss it in public." He wasn't strangling his voice at all now. "I do recognize you, though, and I know you know who I am."

She frowned at him. It was weird to say that he recognized her when they had literally sat beside each other at the meeting. But she had learned over the years that entertainers were often not the most socially adept people, so she didn't mention that.

"I do know who you are," she said, "and I'm not supposed to. Anonymity, remember?"

"Yeah," he said dismissively. "As if that works for people like me."

Well, it usually worked for her, and it probably worked for a bunch of other people on the commission.

He didn't seem to notice her look of consternation. He tilted his head a little, like people did when they were remembering something.

"You worked on the Summertide Theater's outdoor production of *Les Miz*—what? Nine years ago?" He was smiling now, as if happy that the memory had come to him.

"Oh, that," she said. "It was a disaster. You saw it?"

"I was Javert," he said.

She frowned. *"You* were Javert?"

"There was a time when I was not as well known as I am now," he said. "I'm a bona fide local, even though that's been scrubbed off all of my biographies. I like living here. I like spending most of my time here at home with my family."

She was trying to remember the cast. She hadn't interacted with them much, particularly the so-called stars. Everyone on that production was a relative newcomer, all of them starting their careers and jumping at every opportunity they had received.

Except that particular job had not really been the opportunity it had been billed as. She had choreographed the chorus, not as an employee, but as an intern for the professional entertainment company that had rented the venue.

After everything imploded, she had had to jump through all kinds of hoops afterwards with the University of Nevada, Las Vegas to get any kind of credit at all. The internship had been canceled before the company abruptly went out of business, which had caused her all kinds of grief.

She smiled, amused at her younger self. She had

ignored the actors, and really hadn't thought about that production at all once she had survived it.

"I . . . um . . ." She let out a small laugh. "I know it's weird to say now, but I don't remember you. At all."

He laughed—and the laugh was so familiar that a handful of people coming out of one the side doors looked over. Amala knew he had seen them, because his gaze flickered just a bit, but he pretended like they weren't there.

"That's refreshing," he said. "It's kind of ironic, isn't it, that our first interaction was in a production canceled because of weather?"

She blinked and frowned, thinking for a moment. Whenever she considered that terrible experience, it was all overshadowed by the documentation she had to go through, chasing so-called executives who wanted to pretend that they had had nothing to do with the company, which later got sued for millions.

But Ez was right: the original culprit—the reason the production had to close in the first place—had been delays caused by extreme weather.

Extreme weather that no one had planned on. Someone had had the brilliant idea of staging *Les Misérables* in a natural amphitheater in the middle of Death Valley, apparently figuring that there would be no weather troubles in May. Little did the organizers expect that the sets would be ruined by a severe dust storm and just as those were being rebuilt, an early spring monsoon hit, drenching everything, and flooding the amphitheater. There was no way to get the water to recede quickly without the extra expenditure of hiring some company to drain it. When faced with yet another high bill, the production company just shut everything down.

Their insurance didn't pay for the loss either, because no one ever thought about the extremes outside of the weather domes . . . no one except insurance underwriters, that is.

Weather outside the domes was always chancy these days. It had never fully recovered from the Gridlock Era, which meant that May was as windy as March and as suddenly stormy as July.

"You look like you recovered from that loss pretty well," she said, with deliberate irony.

He shook his head, his mouth a thin line.

"I didn't work for a year," he said. "Real work. You know. *My* work."

She did know. She had thought of mentoring rich undergrads in dance after that, but she hadn't. Instead, she had gone onto another internship, this one on the Strip, and that had led to her first real job, and she hadn't stopped working since.

Of course, she didn't make as much money as he did. Besides, only a handful of choreographers in the entire history of the profession had become famous. She doubted she would ever be one of them.

"Want to grab dinner?" he asked.

The invitation surprised her. She had been thinking of food when she came back here, and now, it was clear, so was he.

"Don't you have a show tonight?" she asked.

"We're dark until Thursday. I only do three shows a week."

Such luxury. Three shows a week. Of course, with the crowds he drew, he could do one show a month and probably make back all expenses and then pull in a hefty profit.

"Dinner sounds good," she said, holding up the old-fashioned expenses card she had received that morning. "I only spent half of my allowance."

He laughed. She was beginning to like that laugh.

"I have a third," he said. "We're going to have to go somewhere cheap, because of me."

———— ••• ————————

SOMEWHERE CHEAP TURNED out to be Bugsy's Mobbed Up Sandwich Emporium, which was a local chain. The sandwiches had fun names that actually meant something if someone knew about Las Vegas, like Old Bleu Eyes, made with white bread, mayo, bleu cheese and roast beef. Or the Enforcer, with a small hot pepper in the middle that actually (according to the sandwich description) exploded with taste.

Amala ordered her favorite, the Hole in the Wall, made with a toasted bagel, old-fashioned cream cheese, bacon, and "a good egg." Ez ordered Caesar's Salad Wrap, which seemed light on the lettuce, heavy on the chik'n, and smelled faintly of pepper and anchovies.

They took the sandwiches into the open patio, sitting close enough to the interior to feel some of the air conditioning while feeling like they weren't sitting too close to other tables. Besides, the interior décor was very mob-centric, with pictures of all the old timers, from the little-remembered Moe Dalitz to the truly famous Bugsy Siegel.

By this point, the people that crossed Civic Plaza were the commissioners showing up for their evening shift, and the security guards who checked out whatever the small drones flagged as a problem. Several drones, the size of bumblebees, had flown past the table where Amala sat with Ez, probably attracted by his fame, trying to figure out who, exactly, he was with.

He ignored them completely. She didn't like them, and had no idea how he tolerated it. Constantly being viewed and photographed and recorded, his presence always being broadcast to various media sites, outlets, and private chats. She wouldn't have been surprised if fans showed up demanding his attention or crowding the table.

Only a few did, though, and most of them had clearly arrived for a meeting and were surprised to see him.

Ez was accommodating, gracious in a cool way, and had somehow learned how to finesse a fan out of the area without being rude at all. Mostly, though, people stayed away.

Amala did not ask how he achieved that, but she would if they ever had time alone again. She knew up-and-coming Strip performers who needed to learn how to handle fans as smoothly and easily as he did.

The conversation flowed smoothly. Because the two of them were not allowed to talk about the commission outside of the meeting, they talked about the failed production of *Les Miz* and where their careers went afterwards. They talked about growing up in Las Vegas and how much the city had changed. They talked about the productions they had seen recently and which ones were good.

They laughed more than Amala expected.

Eventually, the sun went down, and the Civic Plaza lights came on, whiter and harsher than the sunlight. It felt later than it was. It also felt like they had been on the patio for several hours, when it had probably been only one.

She hadn't realized she had so much in common with Ez, but they knew the same people and had worked for the same companies. Sure, his career had taken him all over the world, and hers had kept her mostly confined to the States, but that didn't matter. What mattered was this city and the way they had gone from being young, starry-eyed kids with their hands pressed against the glass trying to get in to being insiders who sometimes forgot that they were in a bubble, and that bubble had cost them a lot.

Eventually, it was Amala's legs that made her realize she needed to move. She rarely sat as much as she had on this day. She was usually on the go from the moment she woke up until the moment she fell into bed at night. If she wasn't walking somewhere, she was modeling dance moves or doing some of the choreography herself.

A friend had once referred to her as a butterfly, flicking from one crisis to another, drawing nourishment as she went.

"I'm sorry," she said to Ez. "I need to stand up."

He frowned a little, the way that people who had implanted their clock did, and said, "Yeah, I should get back too. I'm supposed to meet my trainer in an hour."

They both stood and cleared their table, even though it wasn't required. They went back inside. The interior of the restaurant was actually cold after the time on the patio. The two of them seemed to be the only people inside. Someone was clanging around in the back, making sure all the systems from dishwashing to ordering were online, but Amala couldn't see them.

She walked to the public transport kiosk. After a run-in years ago with a dancer who had spectacularly failed an audition and stalked her to, in his words, make her pay for that, she never booked transport from her own connections. The transport logs always kept track of who summoned them, and no matter how hard the services tried, they couldn't easily keep hackers out.

The kiosk was one of the newer ones, which kept track

of all of the nearby services in real time. Apparently, the light rail had reopened after its breakdown this morning, but the system recorded four more breakdowns at nearby stops. Five breakdowns in one day made her leery, but she didn't like taking individual transportation and the underground Vegas Loop stopped too far from her apartment building for a safe walk home.

"I have a transport service," Ez said. "I'm going to call them in a minute. I can drop you somewhere."

Maybe when she knew him better, she would do that, but she had learned even before that stalker-dancer that letting anyone, even seemingly trustworthy people, know where she lived was dangerous. Trustworthy people sometimes casually mentioned where they had met her or dropped her off and that led to problems.

Ez probably had similar problems, but he could probably afford a home with higher levels of security than she could.

"Thanks," she said, "but I'm not that far away."

It was a bit of a lie, but it seemed easier to say than the truth, which was that she didn't trust him. Not yet, anyway.

"Let me walk you to your stop, at least," he said.

She didn't mind that. There was nothing, on either the light rail or on the Vegas Loop, that indicated someone's destination, unlike the Underground in London or the newly revamped subway system in New York.

"All right," she said, and she wiped the public access

screen without choosing the light rail to see when the next train arrived. He would wait with her and she wouldn't be alone on the platform. That would be more than enough.

They left the restaurant, stepping into a completely empty Civic Plaza. The buildings looked larger in the darkness and the plaza itself seemed wider without people scurrying across it. The air had cooled down to a balmy 100 degrees (at least according to her watch)—which wasn't balmy at all, but compared with the sun-drenched high of the morning, it felt like someone had left the air-conditioning on.

At least she didn't immediately fall into a sweat now, although the shirt she was wearing probably had enough salt in it to stand on its own.

Luna had been right; the temperatures felt abnormally high. The media would probably pick up on the mistake that Mirabelle and last July's commission had made. It was only July 1, and the heat already felt unbearable.

Amala couldn't imagine how everyone in the Valley would feel as these temperatures continued throughout the month. And, of course, she hadn't been allowed to ask questions, so she had no idea if the problem that occurred in the meetings last July continued into August.

Amala almost said something to Ez, but thought the better of it. It would probably never be a good idea to discuss the weather with him, because that might lead them into making mistakes, such as talking about the commission as well.

On its west side, Civic Plaza opened onto one of the oldest streets in Las Vegas, which was named, with no originality at all, Main Street. Main was well lit, with cascading lights draped over the roadway from Charleston to Fremont Street.

Directly across from the Civic Plaza was a repurposed parking garage. The backside of the garage formed one of the larger light rail stations, with actual benches. Security patrolled this area, mostly in the form of tiny drones, although there were two guards near the entrance, mostly there to force any vehicles that came inside to take the tacked-on outside ramp. Some city workers had permission to store their personal vehicles in the upper stories of the garage, but the lower level was reserved for the light rail.

Regular railroad tracks ran behind the parking garage, and had been on that site since Las Vegas's founding at the beginning of the 20th century. The railyard was mostly empty now, but occasionally a train rattled by, sounding a bit congested as it did so, since the maglev systems no longer paired well with modern track design.

There were shadows everywhere, despite the extra lights, and not a lot of people. Something moved near the large square opening of the parking garage, probably one of the guards. In the distance, she saw the bright yellow lights that hung over the platform for the light rail. The benches were empty, which pleased her, because she hated being anywhere near the other passengers.

Just beyond it, an old-fashioned train sped by, letting out its distinctive, centuries-old wail. She couldn't see what kind of cars were attached to the back, only that there seemed to be an unusual number of them.

She was about to mention that to Ez when another movement caught her eye. She had a half second to realize that someone was rushing toward her, and then she saw someone else. They were bulky and muscular and they seemed to be holding something strange—a baton or a chain or something.

She didn't have time to parse it out.

"Ez! Look out!" she managed before getting hit from behind.

She staggered forward, the breath knocked out of her from the blow. But she was used to continuing to move even when she was breathless and she did so here, skipping laterally and twirling at the same time.

Two men were coming toward her—but not the two men she had seen emerging from the shadows. Those two were pounding on Ez, who had crumpled into a half crouch, his back the only thing visible.

She danced out of the way of the first man who came at her—he did have a baton and it seemed to sizzle, which told her that it had some kind of charge, something that might incapacitate her.

The other man hung back, as if expecting her to run.

They didn't know her. They didn't know her training.

Besides, there was nowhere to run. Back into the

empty Plaza? She would get trapped. Forward into the light rail station? She would have nowhere to hide.

Sideways down the road? Maybe, if she got free, she could head to Fremont Street, but that only worked if she could run faster than these men, who were bigger than she was.

She had to avoid that baton, which she could do if she was careful. She had had to dance around larger objects than that. The key was stopping these guys, and for that she would have to get dangerously close.

She bobbed under Baton Guy's arm, braced herself, and kicked with all her strength, catching him in the nuts. He gasped and started downward. She hit his baton arm, and the baton clattered to the ground.

For a brief half second, she thought of kicking the baton away, but that would move her out of the strike zone. Instead, she reached up with a clawed hand and shoved her fingers into his eyes.

He screamed, and that was when she realized she hadn't screamed or made any kind of sound. Neither had Ez. This fight was going on in silence, and that wouldn't do.

She needed to scream or yell for help, but she didn't have the breath for it yet.

Baton Guy had fallen to his knees, his hands over his eyes. He wouldn't move for a while.

She needed to get that baton. But first, she had to do something about the second guy. She turned toward him.

He wasn't even looking at her. He seemed panicked as he scrambled for the baton. She took a half a second—maybe less—to assess him. He wasn't a street fighter or a dancer. He had gym muscles and the kind of poor balance that went with it. She would treat him like one of her dancing students.

They moved like he did, all flop and stagger. At the moment, in his panic, he was trying to do too much. He was running and bending over to grab the baton, not thinking about his balance at all.

She danced closer to him, and then kicked him as hard as she could in the ass. He flew forward, just like her clumsiest students did when she shoved them from behind.

He landed several feet from the baton, hard enough to grunt, which meant that the fall had knocked the wind out of him. Some people, though, filled with adrenaline, could overcome that.

She couldn't gamble that he would remain down, so she grabbed the baton. It vibrated with so much charging power that her entire arm shook. It would take an entire class to learn how to use this thing properly.

She was going to have to shut it down just so that she could hold it, but right now, it was ready to go. So she decided to let it do what it did.

She stepped toward the man who was down. He was trying to pick himself up, but slowly, as if he had suffered a greater injury than losing his breath.

She leaned over, and in one fluid, vibrating movement, she stuck the baton against his spine.

He thrashed as if he was in pain. Yellow engulfed him, making him shake as badly as the baton had shaken.

She pulled the baton back, and his shaking stopped. The baton wasn't shaking as much either. Discharging some of its power made it less eager to attack.

But she thrust it at him one more time, more as an experiment than out of any fear or anger. He thrashed again, clearly involuntarily, the yellow making him seem more like a piece of holo art than a human being.

She was hurting him. It took a moment for her to realize that. She was hurting him badly, in the way he had wanted to hurt her.

She pulled back on the baton, and he laid there, immobile.

She couldn't tell if he was breathing or not.

Baton Guy was still rocking, holding his eyes, blood dripping between his fingers onto the pavement. He wasn't going to come after her any time soon. She saw no reason to go after him again.

Behind her, someone yelped.

She whirled. Ez had knocked down one of his attackers, who was struggling to get back up. The other attacker was going after Ez with another baton.

Ez leaned away, ducked, and sidestepped. Amala recognized the stage fencing techniques Ez was using to avoid that baton, and knew he wouldn't last as long as the attacker would.

Neither attacker saw her. She stepped sideways, getting behind the baton attacker. The second attacker was shaking his head, as if he had been hit really hard, but he was still trying to get up. They wouldn't give up. It would only take a minute or two before they subdued Ez.

They didn't notice what she had done to their compatriots. Nor did the security guards inside the light rail station notice either. There was no sound of sirens, so the drones hadn't alerted anyone—not yet anyway. She had no idea how long that would take.

Her arm still vibrated from the baton she was holding, but the vibrations were weaker. She had no idea how long it would hold its charge.

She stepped forward, as silently as she could—light dancer steps—and shoved that baton into the attacker's back.

He froze, outlined in yellow light, mouth open in a silent scream of pain. He didn't vibrate at all. His right arm turned an angry red. The baton he was holding had turned red too, and an alarm blared.

Ez backed up, out of the man's way, and looked on in horror. The fourth man, the one who had been shaking his head, pushed himself off the ground and ran toward Charleston, his footsteps the only sound in the darkness.

Amala's hand ached. She pulled the baton back, and the attacker collapsed bonelessly, his right hand still glowing an alarming red. It looked like his fingers were welded to the baton. He flopped forward, arm extended.

Amala was breathing hard. Her baton seemed to have lost its charge. She wanted to fling it aside, but something cautioned her not to.

She looked at Ez, who looked back at her. They were both stunned.

Sweat ran down her back. The thought *This shirt is ruined* flitted through her mind, and she almost let out an involuntary laugh.

Drones floated above them, clearly recording all of this.

And now, she finally heard sirens, but she had no idea if they were coming here. They sounded very far away.

A security guard stepped out of Civic Plaza, short of breath. He was overweight, his uniform too tight, and she would wager that he had seen none of what had happened, that he had been summoned about the time the drones notified the police.

The guards did not emerge from the light rail station, though, and Amala was beginning to wonder about that. And the empty benches. Had something else happened?

The guard came over, breathing hard, keeping his distance from the three men on the ground, and looking at Amala as if she was the enemy.

"I'm supposed to secure all the weapons," he said, hesitation in his voice. He was at least twice her age, and looked like he couldn't fight a kid's toy punching bag.

"Okay," Amala said, extending her arm. It ached.

The guard ducked, as if she was trying to hit him with the baton.

"I'm trying to give this to you," she said to him. He looked at her warily.

"I'm going to record this," Ez said. He pulled the Weather Commission's phone out of his pocket and punched one of the buttons.

Amala wondered at that. Her emergency implants automatically recorded any situation where authorities had been called. She suspected his did as well.

But he held up the phone like people did in those historical videos from the beginning of the century, when policing was dangerous for people who were not white and privileged.

"Do what you want," the security guard said to Ez.

But the guard continued to stare at the baton Amala was holding out to him. He didn't reach for it at all.

She didn't blame him.

"You know that's illegal, right?" he said, his voice shaking a little.

"I don't even know what it is," she said. "They came at us with them."

She pointedly looked at the baton still in the hand of the third attacker. That man hadn't moved, and the red continued to flare. Bright red lines had worked their way up his arm, and along his shoulder.

"You need to set that down," the guard said. "I don't

think any of us should be touching that. And I'm going to call for an ambulance."

"You don't think the drones called already?" Ez asked with barely contained fury in his voice.

"No, sir, Mr. Oliver, I don't," the guard said. Well, apparently he recognized Ez on sight. "The drones don't call for ambulances. They call law enforcement who then calls for an ambulance. Someone clearly looked at the footage, though, and asked me to secure the scene, and the weapons, which is what I'm doing. But I'm not touching those things. They kill people."

Amala felt a chill run through her, despite the heat. Had she killed those men? She couldn't tell.

"Surely, these men wouldn't want to kill Mr. Oliver," she said.

Ez gave her an irritated look, but she couldn't tell if that was because of what she said or because she too had used his name.

"I don't know what they were trying to do," the guard said. He had his hands out, palms toward her. He had backed away just a little. "Those batons are supposed to subdue people, but if the person has some kind of health issue or something . . ."

His voice trailed off and he looked at the last attacker, the one whose arm was still red. More red lines ran up his face now, illuminating his bones.

"I've never seen anything like that," the guard said, "but I've read about it. It's not good."

It didn't look good. Amala wanted to set her baton down, but right now, she wasn't moving. She didn't want anything she did to seem menacing.

Her heart was pounding. She didn't understand why the authorities hadn't shown up yet. She could hear some sirens. They sounded closer.

She avoided looking at the last attacker. She didn't want to see what had happened to his arm or the rest of him. If she didn't look directly at him, all she saw was a dark red glow on the pavement beside her.

The other attacker, the one Amala had hit first with the baton, was still sprawled. The third one, the one who hadn't been touched with a baton, rocked, keening quietly, the front of his shirt black with streaks of blood.

Sirens were growing louder. There seemed to be even more drones above. Some of them had to be paparazzi drones.

The ache in her arm was profound. Her fingers were wrapped around that baton, which seemed to be vibrating ever so slightly.

Even though the authorities weren't here, she had to get rid of the thing. If the guard wasn't going to take it from her, she needed to set it down.

She crouched, and started to put the baton on the pavement when Ez said, "Don't. The cops are almost here. Let them take it."

"I've got to let go of it," she said.

"There might be a trick to it," Ez said. "And besides, you don't want anyone else to pick it up."

He wasn't looking at the attackers, who still appeared to be out of commission. Instead, he was looking at the guard. She hadn't thought her heart rate could go up, but it had increased to an almost painful drumbeat.

She wasn't sure if that was caused by how much her terror was increasing, or because the baton was somehow hurting her.

Or the idea that Ez implied, which was that the guard might not be who he said he was. Ez would have a lot of experience with people masquerading as someone they were not, and, to be fair, neither he nor Amala had asked for the guard's identification.

The sirens were very close now. Red and blue lights dominated the roadway, and barriers made of yellow caution lights rose around the little tableau in the middle of the road.

Those caution lights also contained sensors, recording the identification of anyone who came through.

Amala was relieved to see the signs of the incoming authorities. Normally she skirted any area where caution lights had gone up. She had certainly never been in the center of them before. But she wanted to get rid of this baton, she wanted out of here, and she wanted to go home.

She suspected that wouldn't happen for a while.

When the caution lights went up, even more drones appeared. Some had the dark blue and gold insignia of the

Las Vegas Metropolitan Police Department. Others were unmarked. Another smaller group had insignias for the various media outlets in Clark County. A handful seemed to have some national insignias as well.

Great. Just great. Her face was probably being broadcast worldwide right now, and here she was, holding an illegal baton.

She stood slowly, feeling lightheaded. She kept that baton extended as far away from herself as she could.

A speed-hover response vehicle arrived almost silently and landed on the Charleston side of the barrier. Two uniformed officers got out. They were tall, and seemed almost as menacing as the men who had attacked her and Ez.

Another speed-hover response vehicle landed, and then another. More officers got out.

The relief that Amala had felt a moment ago faded. Her heart started pounding again. She had no idea if they had watched the footage from the drones. Right now, she was looking like the attacker.

"Mr. Oliver," said one of the first officers, a square-jawed woman who looked sturdy and in shape. "You want to tell us what's going on?"

Annoyance flitted across Ez's face.

"I have not identified myself," he said, clearly identifying himself. Maybe he knew more about the vagaries of the law than Amala did.

Amala didn't care about the niceties. The ache in her arm was growing.

"Can someone take this thing from me?" she asked.

"We have to secure it, ma'am," said another officer. His voice was as deep as Ez's but not as mellifluous.

"Fine," she said. "Just get it away from me."

"You want to identify yourself, then, Mr. Oliver?" the first officer asked. She was standing right next to him.

He turned the ancient phone toward her, and seemed to point it at the badge number written across the shoulder of her uniform.

"I am Ezra Dwight Oliver," he said. "My companion, Amala, and I are the victims here. We demand Victims' Right to Privacy."

The first officer frowned in annoyance, and sighed. Then she turned around and said, "We have to clear all but the Metro drones. The Victims' Right to Privacy has been invoked. All footage needs to be seen and legalities adhered to."

One of the cops still outside the yellow caution lights shook his head as if he did not approve, then stepped back, leaning into the vehicle he had recently exited. Apparently he was taking care of whatever the Victims' Right to Privacy was.

"Okay," Amala said, feeling the heaviness that came after a severe adrenaline rush. She was getting close to collapse. "Can someone take this thing from me? Please."

A different police officer came over to her. It was a

young man who walked with a swagger, the belt on his hips filled with so many different items from guns to batons that he looked like an armory in and of himself.

"You'll have to shut that off," he said.

"I have no idea how," she said. Her voice sounded thick and close to tears. She didn't feel close to tears . . . did she? She was so terrified and lightheaded that she wasn't sure.

"The off command should be keyed to your grip," the officer said.

"Why?" she asked. "It's not my baton."

"Then how did you get it?" He sounded suspicious.

"I picked it up after that guy—" and she nodded at the first attacker, on his knees, doubled over now and still keening, "—dropped it."

"He *dropped* it?" the officer said.

"When I kicked him in the nuts and tried to poke out his eyes," she said.

The officer's eyebrows went up. He glanced at the first attacker, nodded to himself, and then returned his attention to her.

"Then this is going to be harder than I want it to be," the officer said. "I'm going to wait for the med techs to arrive."

Her mouth was dry. Her heart rate was going up from unbearable to she-might-not-have-a-chest-left if someone didn't help her soon.

"Please," she said. "Just get it off me."

"We will, ma'am," he said, but he wasn't looking at her. He was looking at someone outside of the barrier. "I need some assistance here."

Another officer peeled herself away from one of the speed-hover response vehicles and walked through the barrier. She seemed more confident and a bit more aggressive than the officer in front of Amala, although Amala wasn't sure what made her assume that.

She couldn't see Ez anymore. He was surrounded by so many cops that they looked like groupies.

The second officer arrived, glanced at Amala's arm, and then at the officer who had come first.

"It's not hers," he said. "She picked it up off the ground."

"And used it?" the second officer asked.

"Yes," Amala said. "I was defending myself."

She nodded once, frowning at Amala's arm as if it was a problem to be solved.

An ambulance arrived, a long one, the kind they used for big crowd events that had gone awry. Another landed farther away.

Amala saw them, and wanted to wave them over, but she didn't want to move suddenly while she was being studied like this.

"Can the med techs help now?" she asked.

The first officer looked over, saw the techs getting out of the big ambulance and waved them over.

The second officer hadn't moved.

"You used it," she repeated.

"Yes," Amala said. "Please just get it away from me."

"We're trying," the second officer said, even though she hadn't done anything at all. "Did you use it on the man with the baton?"

Amala almost answered *yes*, and then she realized that the second officer meant the attacker who still had a baton, the guy who was glowing red.

"Yes," she said.

"And the two batons interacted," the second officer said, mostly to herself. She walked away without saying anything else to Amala, and headed toward one of the med techs.

They stood near the yellow barrier, changing color as they were hit by rotating red and blue lights.

The second officer was gesturing. The med tech was shaking her head. Not in the way that people did when they disbelieved the person speaking to them, but the way they did when something horrible had happened.

Then the med tech pivoted and headed back to the ambulance. The first officer hovered near Amala.

"What are they doing?" she asked him.

He shook his head slowly, not looking at her at all. The security guard had stepped back, but continued to watch everything. Ez was still filming, but he seemed to be talking softly, which meant he might have been conversing with someone through one of his implants.

Amala was very dizzy and the ache in her arm had turned into actual pain.

"I really am going to need help soon," she said.

"We're getting it, Ma'am," the first officer said, even though he probably knew as little as she did.

Several techs had left the larger ambulance and were coming through the barrier with equipment bags as well as a stretcher. She frowned at them, wondering why they needed so much for her.

But they stopped at the attacker who was glowing red, encircling him. All she could see now was his glow. Two techs from the other, smaller ambulance came through the barrier without as much equipment. One tech crouched over the sprawled attacker, and said something to their compatriot. The compatriot came over and bent down, running a small device over him.

No one came to her, and no one was checking out the injured attacker, who was listing sideways, hands still covering his face. He had stopped keening and was now sobbing quietly.

The second officer came back through the barrier, striding quickly.

"Ma'am," she said when she reached Amala's side. "Follow me."

Then the second officer pivoted and walked back toward the barrier. She stopped just inside of it, not crossing it this time.

Amala could barely keep up. She wasn't sure if it was

the draining adrenaline that caused her inability to move quickly or if something was happening with the baton, but she did not feel like herself.

Two techs came over, both much older than she was. They had weathered skin that implied a lot of time in the weather outside of the dome, and their dark eyes were intense. They didn't introduce themselves, but bent over her arm as if it were something new and different.

Neither of them touched her.

"How long have you been holding the StunStick?" one of them asked.

All Amala could see was the back of the tech's black helmet. She realized then that everyone was in some kind of protective gear except for her.

"That's what it's called?" she asked. "StunStick?"

"Yes," said the person still looking down at Amala's hand. "And it's illegal."

She didn't know how many times people needed to tell her it was illegal. She understood that.

"I just want to let go of it," she said. "Can I let go of it?"

"*No!*" both of the med techs yelled in unison. The officer nearby jumped. The second officer looked over her shoulder. A few of the cops around Ez turned too.

"Just stay still," said the tech who was talking to her. "We'll figure this out."

"What's to figure?" Amala asked. "Please. Let me get out of this. I'm in a lot of pain."

"Yeah," the tech said. "That's what happens when someone who doesn't own the Stick picks it up."

"Great," she said. "Just great."

"So." The tech stood and looked her in the eyes. "How long have you been holding this?"

"I don't know," Amala said. "I wasn't watching any clock. Ez and I were walking from Civic Plaza when these guys jumped us. The security systems probably have it all on file. I really wasn't paying attention to the time."

"She's right," the second tech said. "Get that for us, will you?"

He was looking at the first police officer, who seemed a little annoyed at being instructed by someone outside of the department. He took a step back, so he could talk privately on his links.

The security guard stepped forward. "I was contacted twenty minutes ago," he said. "The fight was underway at that point. I didn't see when she picked up the baton—"

"StunStick," the med tech corrected, but softly.

"—but it couldn't have been more than a few minutes before that."

"Thank you," the other tech said, giving the first a glare. "Less than a half an hour then."

"I think so," the guard said. He looked concerned.

How come everyone knew more about these stick-baton things than Amala did?

"Does that matter?" she asked.

No one answered her, which she heard as a yes. The

techs almost danced around her arm. One of the techs had a tiny black device in her hand, which beeped as she circled it around Amala's wrist.

"Do you know who the owner of the StunStick is?" she asked.

Amala stammered for a moment. The weirdness of the question caught her.

"I fought that guy," she said, and nodded toward the bleeding guy. "He was the one with the baton thingie. He dropped it."

"That makes it easier," the tech said. She looked at the second officer. "Over to you."

The second officer nodded as if she knew what they needed, then headed toward the bleeding guy. No one was helping him, still, which actually bothered Amala, even though she had hurt him.

The second officer didn't touch him either. She removed a small implant reader from her pocket and held it up. Then she beckoned a nearby officer.

Amala couldn't hear what was said, but the second officer gestured at one of the ambulances. The other officer nodded, and headed toward the nearest one, presumably to get some attention for the bleeding guy.

The second officer returned. She turned her implant reader toward the med tech, who tapped the black device in her hand. It beeped again, but the tone was higher, as if it was acknowledging the receipt of something.

"All right," the tech said. "That should be enough to get this off of you."

Apparently, she was speaking to Amala.

"What do you want me to do?" Amala asked.

"Just stay still for a moment," the tech said, "and let me move you."

Whatever that meant. But Amala followed instructions. She didn't move, even though her arm ached worse.

The tech leaned over her, and peeled Amala's pinkie off the baton thingie. The skin on her pinkie stung from the contact, and the bones in her hand throbbed.

"This'll take some time," the tech said, "but we can separate you. I can do it in the ambulance if you want."

"Do you need the equipment from inside there?" Amala asked.

"No," the tech said. Her voice was remarkably calm. "I can do this here."

Amala let out a thin breath. It sounded shaky, maybe because she was shaky.

"Please," she said. "The faster the better."

"This isn't fast," the tech said. "And it will hurt."

"Fine," Amala said. She had no idea what choice she had.

"Make sure none of the fingers I lift off the StunStick touch it again," the tech said. And then she turned her head. "Hey, Collin! I need you."

Another tech looked up, nodded, and came over. They

both bent over her arm, one with some kind of board beneath her and the other working on her fingers.

The pain was exquisite and sharp, located wherever the tech was working. The ache in her arm increased, and her eyes filled with tears.

She didn't blink. Instead, she watched other med techs surround the bleeding guy. They slowly pulled his hands away from his eyes, and one tech looked away, before getting back to whatever they were doing.

Near her, someone screamed in pain, and that seemed to have come from the red glow of the other attacker. No one was helping the sprawled attacker, although one of the police officers now stood near him.

When she had gotten up this morning, and taken the light rail (until it freakin' broke down), she had not expected this. Any of this. And she wasn't sure why it had happened.

All she could think was that they were trying to kidnap Ez, but to what end? No one kidnapped celebrities. Who would pay the ransom? And why?

Pain shot from her forefinger, through her arm, and into her neck. She let out an involuntary *eep!* of pain.

"Sorry," the tech said in a tone that implied she wasn't sorry at all.

The other techs were helping the bleeding guy to his feet. They were supporting him under his arms because it didn't seem like he could walk. The red glow was just as bright, though, and no one had moved from over there.

Another police officer had joined the one near the sprawled man.

Amala didn't see Ez, though. She had no idea if he was even still here. He had been talking to someone, but she didn't know who or why or what was happening.

No one was asking her questions either, just working on the hand attached to that baton-thingie.

She resisted the urge to look down, but she must have moved, because the other tech said, "Stay still. We're nearly done."

They were, too. Her fingers were off the baton-thingie, but her thumb and palm remained on it.

The techs were working on the thumb right now.

"Amala?"

She heard Ez's voice from behind her, and she turned toward him.

"Stop moving!" the tech said in unison.

"Sorry," she said, and returned to the previous position.

"Stop moving!" they said again.

"Sorry." The tears swam in her eyes. She wasn't used to this. She had had a lot of injuries in her career—all dancers did—but never anything like this.

"Don't look at me," Ez said. "I just wanted you to know my lawyer's on the way. She'll deal with the privacy issues."

"Okay," Amala said. She had no idea what the privacy issues were or why she would need a lawyer at all. She was the victim here, and so was Ez. She would ask him as soon as she got free.

Her thumb was free now, so all that remained was her palm, pressed against the baton-thingie. The techs were no longer trying to lift her hand away from the thingie; they were trying to separate it from her skin.

She could feel a sharp little tool scratching away at the connection. She made herself concentrate on what she saw —the bleeding man trying to stagger as the techs led him to the other ambulance. He left behind a trail of wet that was probably blood but looked like oil, changing color with the reds and blues and yellows of the various lights.

One of the cops near the sprawled man was gesturing at a third cop who had just showed up. He started to crouch, holding some flex cuffs, when the first cop stopped him and said something. Then the second cop beckoned the techs.

Apparently someone had finally decided to give the sprawled man medical attention.

"There!" the first med tech said, standing up. "You're free."

It took Amala a moment to understand that the tech was talking to her.

"I can move?" she asked.

"Yes," the tech said.

The other tech had the baton-thingie on the board. The baton was in a little groove that the board seemed to have carved into itself just to hold it all.

The first tech was encasing Amala's arm in some kind of cooling gel. It made the ache less fierce. The skin of her hand still stung, though, but not as severely as it had earlier. Now, it felt like she had grabbed a metal pole in the middle of winter with her bare hand and pulled away too quickly.

"Come with me," the tech said. "We'll get you examined in our portable hospital."

So it wasn't a big giant ambulance afterall. It was a mobile medical unit. Amala had no idea the Vegas Valley had one of those.

The tech started forward, then looked back to see if Amala was following. She was, but she felt unsteady, as if she had danced a difficult four-hour solo show without taking any kind of nourishment or liquid at all.

The tech came back, hovering near her as if asking permission to help her. Amala really didn't want anyone touching her aching body.

"I'll make it," she said.

The tech nodded, and then stepped away, walking sideways so she could keep an eye on Amala.

They had to go around the clump of techs around the red glow. Some other police officers were on the scene now, doing things that Amala couldn't see well. One of them was talking to the guard.

Most of the drones had backed away, but a large one hovered overhead.

"We don't need you, sir," the tech said suddenly, and Amala looked sideways.

Ez was walking with them.

"I'm coming anyway," he said. "I don't think Amala and I should be separated right now."

Amala frowned at him, not sure why he felt that way. But she was not thinking as clearly as she wanted to be right now.

"Are you family?" the tech asked. "Because we might need to get her to the hospital and only family—"

"I will be with her," Ez said. "My lawyer will be here soon if you have questions."

The tech shook her head as if she couldn't quite believe what she had heard. But she didn't say anything more, just walked to the big mobile medical unit.

Amala frowned at it, wondering why the authorities had deemed that thing necessary with this attack.

But she didn't ask, figuring that the tech wouldn't know. She followed the tech inside, with Ez right behind them, and braced herself for whatever was going to come next.

———— ••• ————

HOSPITALS, mobile or otherwise, were apparently very much the same. Amala was used to getting scans and seeing holo imagery of injuries. The dead connecting tissue in her hand startled her, but the emergency doctor inside told her that repairs would be relatively painless, considering how quickly they had found and solved the problem.

He had spent most of their time together flitting back and forth between talking with her, doing the work to see if her fingers still worked, and checking other monitors.

It took her a few minutes to realize that the other monitor was focused on the red glow of a human being still face down on the closed-off street.

She was in the emergency medical unit for more than an hour. The doctor gave her some kind of nanorepair something or other that she didn't entirely understand. Half of her brain had checked out, and she was trying desperately to get it to return. She wasn't sure how to do that.

Fortunately, Ez had recorded the entire conversation and promised to send it to her.

She had the required recording that the medical unit made of the treatment as well, and an appointment in the morning (*If you can make it*, the ER doc said, sounding like he knew she might be busy with something else) with a specialist who dealt with hand injuries caused by StunSticks.

"We might be able to find you a better specialist," Ez had said after the ER doc went back to check on his other patient. Amala wasn't sure why Ez felt responsible for her, but she was glad he was there.

"Okay," Amala said. At that moment, her brain was whirring, and she needed to slow down. Too much was happening. One specialist or another, it mattered, but right now, she needed to get out of here and do—what, she wasn't sure.

When they finally stepped out of the mobile medical unit—Amala with a bag of painkillers she would probably never take and some healing medication that she would, and Ez with all kinds of documentation, official and otherwise—the heat had gathered around them like it had been waiting for them.

The caution lights were still on, but most of the speed-hover response vehicles were gone. Other official-looking vehicles had arrived and were positioned outside of the caution lights. Some of the figures inside the lights were shadowy. They had their own lights as they surveyed the ground where the confrontation had happened.

The entrance to the light rail station was blocked off with more caution lights, and that gave Amala a chill despite the heat. The attackers had come from that direction, but this seemed like something more than that.

She felt like this entire evening had been monumental in ways she didn't understand.

"Amala," Ez's voice was soft, and brought her back to herself. She was blocking the entrance to the mobile medical unit. She stepped away from the entrance, not sure where she should go.

If the light rail was shut down, then how was she going to get home?

"Amala," Ez said again. He was to her right, and as she turned in that direction, she realized he wasn't alone.

A woman stood beside him, glowing softly in the caution lights. She was taller than he was, taller than Amala as well, and wore a black suit like the women who had been in the meeting that morning (which felt like 300 years ago). The suit seemed more expensive though, and it caught the light, almost as if there were sparkles built into the fabric.

Amala stopped up short, not sure what was going on. She wished her brain wasn't overwhelmed with residual pain, extra meds, and the heaviness that came after unusual exertion.

"Amala," Ez said, "this is my attorney, Deidre Koppelstein."

Koppelstein. Everyone in the Valley would recognize that name. It headed one of the biggest and most prestigious law firms in Nevada. It was emblazoned as a sponsor for every single charity promotion that happened in the city, and appeared in the media all the time, generally for high-profile cases that resulted in high-profile wins.

"Hi," Amala said. "I'd shake your hand, but—"

"I don't do that anyway," Koppelstein said, but not in an offensive way. Almost forgiving, as if Amala had made some kind of faux pas. "It's a pleasure to meet you."

Koppelstein had a long, angular face, and dark eyes that matched her stunningly glossy dark hair. Her hands had the kind of manicure that Amala couldn't have gotten if she wanted to; one hour at her job and those nails would have shattered.

"It's a pleasure to meet you too," Amala said, relying on manners that she had learned in her extremely strict childhood. She had always defaulted to those when she was completely exhausted.

"I'm going to be handling you in this case for convenience," Koppelstein said. "Unless you have other representation . . .?"

"Case?" Amala asked. She willed herself to think clearly. She had to focus. Events were moving too fast for her to allow herself to sink into a blessedly numb mental fog.

"You were attacked and you were injured. We're not sure what is going on here, but initially, the police thought you were a perpetrator because of the StunStick."

Koppelstein had a strong voice that seemed to grow even more assured as she spoke about the case.

"I'm not a perpetrator of anything," Amala said. She didn't like how weak her voice sounded. "I was having dinner with—"

"I already told her," Ez said. "We're getting the drone footage now. It'll prove that you had nothing to do with the attack."

"There were drones everywhere on the Plaza," Amala

said. "I thought maybe they were paparazzi drones, but I didn't—"

"I've already got footage from the meal. I'm pretty sure that's how the attackers found Ezra." Koppelstein smiled. "I have a large staff. We have most of this under control."

"Most of . . ." Amala repeated.

"There are things we don't entirely understand," Koppelstein said. "Usually fans and stalkers don't attack a celebrity. So this is some kind of plot or something. Metro is searching for the surviving attacker, the one who fled, and they believe they will get information from the one you stunned."

"I stunned two of them," Amala said.

"Yes, well, the one that they were able to move. He's injured but waking up. You did a good job, by the way." Koppelstein threw out the compliment as if it were a piece of candy and Amala was a hungry six-year-old.

"We have no idea why they came after me," Ez said, "but we'll find out. I'm sorry you got caught in the middle of it, though. Don't worry. I'll handle the legal expenses, and medical ones if you need that."

He was clearly offering because he was afraid she would sue him, the celebrity with deep pockets. She wouldn't do that, but she had no idea how to tell him that.

Default politeness almost made her decline. She had great insurance through her work, but she had no idea what this all would entail. Nor did she know if the injury would interfere with her work.

Usually that wasn't a problem, because dancers got injured all the time and were covered, and so were the choreographers. But this was the first time she had been injured *off* the job. She had no idea how they would react to it.

They already weren't pleased that she had taken on three separate months for her civic duty, although by law, they weren't supposed to complain about that.

So, instead of refusing his offer, she said, "Thank you."

"Good," Koppelstein said. "That's settled. We'll have you sign documentation on the way to Metro."

The need to sign documents Amala understood. If they were going to have an agreement and Ez was going to help her legally, then documents had to be signed.

But Metro?

"I'm sorry," Amala said, not sure if she understood correctly. "We're going to Metro? Why?"

"I promised the officer in charge of the scene that we'd go to Metro as soon as you were done in the mobile medical unit," Koppelstein said.

"Why, exactly?" Amala said. They had been on the scene. Someone had taken her statement. They had seen what had happened with that baton thingie. Plus the drones recorded everything.

"I'd like to say it's a formality," Koppelstein said, "but

it is not. You were injured, which is something I care about—"

"Me, too," Ez said quietly.

"—and so were three other people."

"Attackers," Amala said. "The *attackers* were injured."

"Yes, they were," Koppelstein said. "Two of them severely."

"And Metro wants to charge me with this?" Amala had to work to keep her voice level. "This was self-defense."

"It was clearly self-defense," Koppelstein said. "And at some point, you're going to have to share with me who trained you like that, because I might send clients to them."

Amala couldn't tell if that comment was some kind of b.s. said to make her feel better or if Koppelstein meant what she said.

"Then what do they want to talk with me about?" Amala asked. She wasn't going anywhere with anyone whom she had just met, even if that person had said she was a lawyer. Not with some kind of weird demand from Metro.

"They don't have your story entirely," Koppelstein said. "Besides, I want them to talk with you."

That sounded strange. "Why?"

Ez started to speak but Koppelstein put a hand on his arm.

"Because we are going to go after these attackers with the full force of the law," Koppelstein said. "We want people to know they can't come after any celebrity in this town, particularly Ezra Oliver."

Amala shot a sideways glance at Ez. He looked exhausted and concerned at the same time.

"To do that," Koppelstein said, "we have to cooperate as much as possible with the police investigation."

"And you want me wrapped up in this so that . . . what? . . . I cooperate?"

"You are part of it," Koppelstein said. "We really want to help you, especially on the medical side. But that's your choice."

Choices, when Amala was this injured, and at this time of night, after one of the longest days of her life. She was going to have to make decisions, and she had no one to confide in.

But the painkillers had kicked in. They had reduced the ache in her arm, but it remained. She could barely feel her hand at the moment.

She recognized the feeling of a nerve block, and knew that once it wore off, she would be in breathtaking amounts of pain.

Until then, though, she would have some clarity, if she chose to use it.

Koppelstein must have seen the hesitation on Amala's face.

"I know it's a lot," Koppelstein said. "You're up for

this, right? Because if not, we can take you home. The police will want to speak to you eventually, and I would like to be there. My theory is the sooner the better, but if you're not ready—"

"I'm up for it," Amala said, even though she wasn't certain what she was up for. All she knew was that she wanted to end this nightmare as soon as she possibly could.

"We'll get you home as quickly as possible," Ez said, as if he could make that promise.

"Thanks," Amala said, as if she believed him.

Then they walked—ever so slowly, because of her—to a large vehicle that was hugging the curb. Amala had seen dozens of vehicles like this after she'd gotten her first job on the Strip. When she'd been in college, she'd laughed at anyone who rode in one because the vehicles were big and pretentious. Then she learned about the safety features, not just providing protection from injuries in an accident, but providing protection against surveillance, stalkers, and paparazzi.

As she got into the back of the vehicle behind Ez and Koppelstein, she ran through the various options that she had. She would see how this meeting went at Metro . . . and if she needed her own representation.

Although she knew this would do for now.

———— ••• ————

THE LAS VEGAS Metropolitan Police Department's headquarters were ancient. Recessed behind what had been a parking lot back when everyone owned their own vehicles, the building covered several city blocks. Wings had been tacked on over the decades, taking what might have been a nice old-fashioned façade into a Frankenstein's monster of a building, one that required floating signage for anyone to find their way around the inside or outside.

Koppelstein's vehicle stopped in front of a side door that Amala hadn't even noticed in her handful of visits to Metro. She had had to come to the building when she came of age, like everyone, to have an official identity implant added. Then she had come back to have it updated when the technology changed while she was in college.

The first time, she hadn't gotten lost because her parents knew where they were going, but every succeeding time—including the time she had come with an attorney to press charges against her stalker—she had gotten turned around despite the floating signage.

Koppelstein, however, seemed to know where she was going. She got out on the far side of the vehicle, and Ez followed her. Amala clutched her arm and somehow managed to follow them, thankful that she was in good enough shape that she didn't need her arms to brace her for that movement.

She did feel the echoes of pain along her right side,

though, and knew that she would eventually find even this simple movement difficult.

The air seemed cooler away from the downtown corridor, but that might simply have been a function of the hour. She hadn't checked the time since she got out of the mobile medical unit, but she knew it had to be late.

Koppelstein closed the door behind Amala, as if hurrying her along, then swept a hand toward the building itself. Amala took a few steps and waited, because she wasn't going to get trapped in that maze again.

Apparently, Koppelstein understood, because she said, "Follow me," and marched forward without checking where Ez and Amala were.

They followed, Ez staying by her side, and stepped up a curb onto a cracked sidewalk that needed repair. Weeds struggled to break through those cracks, almost like tiny decorations. Weeds were not something she was used to; they had been abolished by rigid exterior appearance laws on the Strip decades ago.

Floating signs appeared in front of Amala's eyes asking where she wanted to go.

"Crap," Ez said. "We got a visual distraction, Deidre."

"Oh, sorry," she said, and did something with a tiny device in her right hand that Amala hadn't noticed before. The floating signs vanished, leaving reverse images in front of her eyes.

Koppelstein then opened the door, and waited as both Ez and Amala went through.

The air smelled of sweat and malfunctioning air conditioning. The AC unit—whatever it was—struggled to keep the temperature at a comfortable level, not assisted by the depth of the indoor humidity.

The lighting in here was more brown than yellow, probably because the fixtures were as old as the building itself. The door was clearly a side door because it opened into a small area only a few feet from a flight of stairs.

Ahead, voices echoed, some of them familiar. Amala wasn't sure why there would be familiar voices here, unless her very good musical ear had focused enough on the various officers that had spoken to her to recognize their voices this quickly.

Koppelstein went up the stairs quickly, veering to her right. Ez waited for Amala, who took the stairs slowly, feeling the jostling on her side.

Maybe it had been a bad decision to come here. She was in worse shape than she had thought.

The floor they arrived on was flat and dated. There were desks separated by those antique barriers that businesses used around the turn of the century, usually to tack papers to. These barriers did have paper items tacked to them, but these items were so old that they had yellowed and in some instances, the bottoms were curling.

Most of the desks were cluttered with devices and bags of what she could only assume were evidence or other important matters. Chairs were pushed against some of the desks and others had a person leaning over an ancient tablet, poking at them.

An office stood at the end of the row of desks. The office had a glass wall and a cluster of people inside. The door was open.

That was where Koppelstein was heading. Ez stayed beside Amala, hand out as if he expected her to fall.

"I'm okay," she said, more because his closeness irritated her than because it was true.

He nodded, but didn't respond. They walked together toward that open door. The office was the source of all the familiar voices. Several people stood inside, hands waving, as if the conversation had gotten intense.

Koppelstein stood outside the room, just barely, and rapped her knuckles on the door.

The sound stopped the discussion.

"I'm Deidre Koppelstein," she said. "I represent Ezra Oliver and Amala Navarro. They are here to make their statement."

"Well, they'll have to work with our attorney," said a voice that Amala recognized. She'd been listening to it all day.

"Mirabelle," she said softly to Ez. "What's she doing here?"

He shook his head. They finally reached the door. The name plate plastered along the side stated that the office belonged to a deputy chief. Amala had to assume that person was the man standing behind the room's tiny desk, an annoyed expression on his face, arms crossed.

"I have no idea why Mirabelle is here," Ez said. "This night is getting weirder and weirder."

It was.

Amala stayed outside of the room, but close enough to the door so that she could hear. Ez went a little farther in, and people parted for him. Some of them tried not to look at him, pretending his celebrity didn't bother them. Others stared openly at him.

Amala didn't recognize all of the people, but Mirabelle looked the same as she had that morning, except that her blue caftan was wrinkled. Next to her stood a short, sharp-eyed woman in an ill-fitting brown suit.

"I would like my clients in and out of this building quickly," Koppelstein said easily, as if she were asking for a cup of coffee. And yet the demand had teeth. Amala had never heard that kind of casual pressure from anyone before.

"I can't guarantee quickly," the deputy chief said. He had turned toward Koppelstein, and seemed to be talking to her as if she was the only person in the room.

"You can try," Koppelstein said with a bit more edge. "Amala has been injured. She needs rest."

The deputy chief looked over at Amala. There was a slight frown between his dark eyes. It was almost as if he hadn't really seen her before.

She resisted the urge to raise her injured arm in acknowledgement of his gaze. Instead, she met it evenly.

"I'll do my best," he said, "but Deidre, this attack is odd."

"I can see that," Koppelstein said. "People were injured."

"People have *died*," he said.

Amala's breath caught. "Who died?" she asked.

No one looked at her, but Ez said softly, "The last guy, the one who was still on the ground when we left."

The one who was glowing red. Of course he had died. No one could live through that.

Her eyes filled. She wasn't sure how she felt about actually killing someone, even if it had been to save her own life.

"My clients were defending themselves," Koppelstein said. It was amazing the way she kept adding edges to her voice, as if she knew what each layer represented and how effective that layer would be.

"I didn't say they weren't." The deputy chief seemed a bit tense. "It's just—"

"There is no 'just' anything," Koppelstein said. "I've seen footage, you've seen footage. They were talking and laughing when those men came across the street and started assaulting them with weapons."

"I *know*," the deputy chief said.

"That's the definition of self-defense," Koppelstein said.

Amala felt a chill run through her. Was someone thinking of charging her with murder? Because she defended herself.

She felt lightheaded, and for a moment, she blamed the medication. Then she realized she hadn't been breathing. She forced herself to inhale slowly and then exhale softly.

"If you're thinking of going after my clients," Koppelstein said, "then we are leaving right now."

"I am not," the deputy chief said. "You're not letting me finish."

"We're the ones who've been arguing," Mirabelle said, butting in.

Amala almost rolled her eyes. Amazing how just one day's experience had made her despise Mirabelle.

"I've seen the footage too," Mirabelle said. "This isn't about celebrity. This is about the commission."

Koppelstein gave Mirabelle a withering look and then turned her attention back to the deputy chief.

"I didn't ask," Koppelstein said, her voice now filled with an ever-so-slight tinge of contempt, "but who *are* these people?"

"I'm Mirabelle—"

The deputy chief held up his hand. "Mirabelle, whose last name I am not allowed to give to you," he said to Koppelstein, but clearly that last bit was a reminder spoken to Mirabelle herself, "chairs the Weather Commission."

Koppelstein raised an eyebrow. "The *Weather* Commission?"

"Yes." The deputy chief waited.

Ez cursed under his breath. Apparently, he hadn't told Koppelstein what he had been doing downtown.

Koppelstein glared at him from across the office. "That's your civic duty?" she said. "What were you thinking? I could've gotten you a day-long assignment or figured out how to move—"

"Not here, Deidre," the deputy chief said. "We tend to frown on those who ignore the civic duty around here and frown harder when they work to get out of it."

"I've lived here my entire life," Ez said. "I *like* it here. And Vegas is all about weather, so I thought—"

"You *thought?*" Koppelstein said, as if thinking was a bad idea. "What did you think?"

"That it would be interesting. And it even said in the pitch that anonymity was important." Ez swallowed.

"Yes, anonymity was important," Koppelstein said. "So that's why it's a bad idea for a famous person to join the commission."

Ez's cheeks turned a slight shade of red.

"We've had famous people on the commission before," Mirabelle said. "Everyone wants a piece of the weather. And that's the issue."

She planted her solid self a little ahead of the other woman near her, and said, "I've seen this before, chief."

"Really?" he said. "Because I checked. We haven't

had an attempted kidnapping in this area in a long time. Certainly not one of high-profile people. We still have a problem with human trafficking near the airport, but we're working on that—"

"You're not listening, chief," the short woman in the wrinkled brown suit said. "This is about the Weather Commission."

"And you are . . .?" Koppelstein asked as if it were her office and not the deputy chief's.

"Anita Glower," the woman said. "I'm the lawyer whose lucky task it is to represent the Weather Commission."

She didn't sound like she felt lucky. She sounded like a woman who didn't like her job at all. Or maybe she just didn't like Mirabelle.

"Anita, look," the deputy chief said, "I've told you before, you need to take some of these issues up with the Civic Duty Authority."

"I have," she said, "and they sent me back to you, or don't you recall our discussion last week?"

The deputy chief sighed theatrically. "I do recall," he said with exaggerated patience. "We have a team who investigates all bribery contacts connected to your commission and every other commission. If *you* recall, we arrested the chair of the SandsDune Retail Resort for his repeated attempts to get the temperatures lowered in the summer."

"You think it ridiculous, I know," Glower said, "but if

people know that Las Vegas summers aren't as brutal as they used to be, then our summer tourism will increase. That's worth millions."

Mirabelle had stepped back slightly. Now it was her cheeks that had flushed. Apparently she had received that lecture as well.

A thin man in a t-shirt and a pair of cut-offs stopped near Amala. She leaned closer to Ez so that the man wouldn't touch her injured arm.

For a moment, she thought the man had come to see Ez. A few other employees of the department were lurking around the office, apparently trying to see the celebrity.

But this guy didn't even seem to notice Ez.

The deputy chief clearly wasn't concerned with anything going on at the edges of his office door. Instead, he was looking directly at Glower.

"I doubt the Retail Board or anyone connected with Las Vegas Tourism or the hospitality industry would send thugs to make their point," the deputy chief said. "So, let's treat this for what it is. An assault on one of our citizens—"

"Two," Amala said before she could stop herself.

Koppelstein gave her a small, approving smile.

"What I meant," the deputy chief said, "is that this is an unusual event, and we will treat it as such."

"Chief," the thin man near the door said. "If I may . . .?"

Uncertainty crossed the deputy chief's face for just a

moment. Then the look vanished. "Need to speak to me in private, Detective?"

"No, sir." The thin man opened his hands as if he wasn't sure what he wanted. "I mean, maybe. I mean, it's up to you."

Amala had never seen anything like this man. She had met detectives before, usually investigating something bad that had happened on the Strip, and most of them looked like Anita Glower—unkempt and easily dismissible until they opened their mouths.

This man looked like he had ironed his t-shirt, his cut-offs and the pure white socks tucked into his very clean shoes. All of that suggested precision.

"We went through layers of identification," the detective said, "but it was the DNA on the dead subject that helped us."

The deputy chief stood very still. Amala couldn't tell if he was regretting not talking to the detective in private.

"We're not dealing with the Retail Board or some random business owner who wants to know what the weather will be in advance so he can make more money selling indoor vacations," the detective was saying. "These are Anti-Domers."

It took a moment for Amala's tired brain to understand what he meant. Anti-Domers, a fringe group that had opposed the weather domes since they were adopted decades ago. Anti-Domers believed that human beings should live with the results of their near-destruction of Earth's climate, and worked on changing that.

"What the hell would they want?" Koppelstein asked. "This was an *attack*, and—"

"It was an attempted kidnapping," Glower said, as if she was in charge of the room. "Think of the leverage they would have gotten if they had Ezra Oliver, a newly minted member of the Weather Commission. Think of what they would have asked for."

Ez shivered visibly. Amala's mouth was dry.

"We've been telling you," Glower said to the deputy chief. "Our commission has been receiving threats."

"Vague threats," the deputy chief said almost absently as he frowned at the detective.

"Serious threats," Glower said, "that have led to some commissioners resigning."

"What do they want?" Koppelstein asked. "It is my understanding that the Weather Commission has nothing to do with whether or not there's a dome at all."

"It was an opportunity, because Mr. Oliver is so recognizable," the detective said. "We've been receiving chatter for months from the Feds saying that a big action has been planned against weather domes all over the country. Imagine if they started with the kidnapping and murder of Mr. Oliver?"

"Jesus," Ez said. His skin had gone gray.

"Then that's how we take care of this," Koppelstein said. "We will let news outlets and all the media sites know that Ezra and his companion responded quickly and thwarted a terror attack on the city, and we will call on the authorities—"

"Amala did," Ez said. "Amala thwarted the attack, not me. I was just flailing—"

"No offense, Ezra," Koppelstein said, "but a random woman stopping the attack—"

"Is bad-ass," he said.

Amala stepped away, found a chair and sat down heavily. She was lightheaded and she needed to breathe. She needed to recover. She needed to see the damn specialist.

She didn't want to be famous for anything, not even for being bad-ass.

"What do you say about that, Amala?" Ez was asking. He was looking around until he saw her. "We put you out there for your heroics—"

"No," she said quietly. "No."

"This news will get out," Ez said, "and when it does—"

"When it does," Amala said, "people will be afraid to sit on any commission. We can't let that happen. That'll lead to chaos. It'll harm the very system we set up to make sure everything ran smoothly after the days of gridlock."

She had initially said no for herself, but as she spoke, she found herself impassioned about this.

"She's got a point," Koppelstein said, nodding toward Amala. "I hadn't thought of that. Forget what I said, chief. We're going to pretend this didn't happen at all. Ezra already asked for his Victim's Right to Privacy to be respected. Those need to include Amala. If you release any information on this attack, you will not name the victims."

Ez let out a small breath, as if that calmed him.

"I'm going to take my clients, and go," Koppelstein said. "If you need them as witnesses in any legal proceedings, you'll contact my office and we'll negotiate how to maintain their anonymity."

The deputy chief sighed. "All right," he said. "You'll have to leave then. Because this will be a legal conversation your clients can't hear."

"Fine," Koppelstein said. "We will be talking with the city about protection for its commissioners. The fact that there have been threats makes this attack and the damage to my client's arm preventable, had they had the proper security."

"Deidre, we don't need that," the deputy chief said. "We're handling things."

"Clearly you're not," she said. She pushed her way out of the room.

Amala watched her in silence, thinking that Koppelstein had a different kind of defensive force, one that made her seem incredibly formidable in ways that Amala never would.

"Wait!" the voice belonged to Mirabelle. Of course.

She trailed after Koppelstein, looking alarmed.

"This means your clients aren't going to be on the

commission anymore. And we're not going to be able to meet until we get someone new. We can't have that." Mirabelle looked panicked. "It's July, after all."

Koppelstein peered at her. "What does July have to do with it?"

"Don't ask," Ez said, moving forward far enough to physically block any conversation between the two women. "And yes, we're leaving the commission."

"No," Amala said, almost before he finished the sentence. "I'm not."

Everyone looked at her. She supposed she understood the shock on all of their faces. If anyone should resign, it was her. But that would have meant her injury was for nothing.

"I've only been doing this for one day," she said, "but what's happening with the Weather Commission is a nightmare and it needs to be fixed."

She stood up, swayed and looked at Glower, who was still in the chief's office.

"You work for the commission, right?" Amala said.

Glower frowned at her. "Yes."

"Then you're going to work with me. We're going to petition the Civic Duty Authority for security and background checks and protection for commissioners as long as they serve. And increased pay to make this worthwhile."

"The pay rate for commissioners—"

"Is the same across the commissions, I know," Amala

said. Her lightheadedness was getting worse. She was almost out of energy. "But if we're asking commissioners to work under threat of attack or to have to deal with criminals set on bribing them or to negotiate threats, we need to compensate them for that."

Her words echoed in the large room. No one spoke or even moved.

She looked at Koppelstein. "You're going to help with this too," Amala said. "This is a flaw in the system and we have to fix it. Now, before anyone else gets hurt."

Koppelstein looked at her, and then at Ez. "I don't think—"

"Oh, c'mon, Deidre," Ez said. "You love a challenge. This will be one."

"I'm in charge of the commission," Mirabelle said in a small voice. "You have to go through me—"

"Oh trust me," Ez said. "I think she will. And I want to watch. I've changed my mind. I'm staying."

"Ezra . . ." Koppelstein said, her incredibly expressive voice filled with warning. "That's not a good idea."

"Oh, I think it's a great one," he said. "I'm tired of being a show pony. Let's do something important for a change."

Koppelstein shook her head just a little. Mirabelle looked like she had eaten something bad, but Glower was smiling ever so slightly.

Amala noted all of that through swimming vision. The energy from all the medication was failing her.

Her knees gave out and she sank back into the chair.

"All right," Koppelstein said, and then beckoned some officers who were still watching Ez. "Let's get her home, since she has a meeting tomorrow."

Oh, fun, Amala thought. That was just what she needed. "After I see the specialist," she said.

"Yes," Koppelstein said. "We'll make sure you do everything you need to tomorrow."

And as Amala let the officers help her up, she realized she trusted Koppelstein to do that. Amala trusted all of it.

And she was actually looking forward to it.

She didn't think that was the medication talking.

"Why are you staying?" she asked Ez as he flanked her on the way out.

"Because you're badass," he said, "and I like watching you work."

Then he smiled at her—that famous Ezra Oliver smile. It shouldn't have made her feel better, but it did.

She had a lot to unpack, and she would. But first, she needed rest. And then she had a mission.

She'd never had one before. Before she had drifted between what was expected of her and what she did for work. Now, she felt like she could actually make a difference.

And it felt good.

BUT WAIT, THERE'S MORE!

Want more masterful science fiction?

Go to wmgbooks.com!

Sign up for the Kristine Kathryn Rusch newsletter, and keep up with the latest news, releases and so much more—even the occasional giveaway.

To sign up go to kriswrites.com

Get the latest news and releases from all of WMG's authors and lines, including Kristine Grayson, Kris Nelscott, *Pulphouse Magazine,* and so much more…

To sign up, **go to wmgbooks.com.**

ABOUT THE AUTHOR
KRISTINE KATHRYN RUSCH

Kristine Kathryn Rusch sold more than 35 million books worldwide. She publishes bestselling science fiction and fantasy, award-winning mysteries, acclaimed mainstream fiction, controversial nonfiction, and the occasional romance.

Her novels made bestseller lists around the world and her short fiction appeared in more than twenty best-of-the-year collections. She won more than twenty-five awards for her fiction, including the Hugo, *Le Prix Imaginales*, the *Asimov's* Readers Choice award, and the *Ellery Queen Mystery Magazine* Readers Choice Award.

To find out more about her work, go to her website, kriswrites.com

facebook.com/kristinekathrynruschwriter

patreon.com/kristinekathrynrusch

bookbub.com/authors/kristine-kathryn-rusch